HOW THE MOON BEGAN

A folk tale from Grimm
adapted by

JAMES REEVES

Illustrated by

EDWARD ARDIZZONE

Abelard-Schuman

© 1971 by James Reeves and Edward Ardizzone
First published in 1971 in Great Britain
First published in 1972 in the USA
I.S.B.N. 0 200 71862 2 (Trade)
I.S.B.N. 0 200 71867 3 (GB) (USA only)
L.C.C.C. No. 72-169201

How the Moon Began

This is the story of how the moon began. Once upon a time there was no moon. The nights were as black as black. If you went out without a lantern, ten to one you bumped into somebody else. So people gave up going out at night and stayed at home. Usually they went to bed as soon as the sun disappeared behind the mountains.

Now there was no blacker place at night than the land of Exe. One fine morning, bright and early, four men of Exe set out to do business in the land of Wye. They were brothers. The first one's name was Arn, which means "the old one".

The second one's name was Bor, which means
"the quiet one".

The third one's name was Cass, which means "a man of deeds";

and the fourth one's name was Deol, which means "cunning" or "crafty".

When the four men of Exe had done their business in Wye, they started for home. Soon the sun went down, and night overtook them. But the night was

not dark, as in their own country. Nor was it as
bright as day. It was half-and-half—light enough for
the four men to see each other and to see their way.

"'Tis a very bright night for the time of day,"
said Arn. "Very different from home. What be the
cause of it, Brother Bor?"

Bor said nothing, but Cass said, "There is a light
over there, right above yonder oak tree."

"That is a very clever contraption," Deol said,
nodding his head wisely.

"Aye, that it is," Arn said. "What can it be,
I wonder?"

In the soft light that shone all round them they
saw a man of Wye approaching.

They stopped him, and Cass said, "What is that
light, sir? It seems to be a very good light."

"Ah," replied the man of Wye, "that is the moon. Our Mayor bought it for two pounds ten and hung it up over that oak tree. It lights up the whole country. We have to pay him six and eightpence a

week to fill it with oil and keep it clean, so that it burns steady all night."

"Thank you, sir," said Deol, "and goodnight to you."

"Let us take this moon," said Arn. "The people of Wye can very well buy another one for themselves, and this is exactly what we need back home. We have an oak tree just as good as this one, and there we will hang it to enlighten the whole of Exe."

"You are right, Brother Arn," Cass said. "You and Deol go and find a cart, while Brother Bor climbs into the tree to fetch this moon down. Brother Bor is just the man to climb to the top of the tree."

So Arn and Deol went to fetch a cart, while Bor clambered into the tree, cut a hole in the lamp and passed a rope through it.

He and Cass lowered it to the ground, and together the four brothers lifted it into the cart. Then
they covered the shining ball with their cloaks so
that no one could see what they had stolen. With
two of them in front of the cart and two at the back,
they pushed it home to the land of Exe.

They hung it on the top of a tall oak tree, and everyone in Exe was delighted with their new lamp.

The soft light shone into sitting rooms and bedrooms, so that no one had to go to bed in the dark; and if a man went out at night, he no longer bumped into his friends. The dwarfs came out of their caves in the mountains and ran races with the rabbits.

The elves in their red pointed caps danced in rings on the village green. The four brothers took care to see that the moon was kept clean and full of oil, and

was lit every night as the sun went down. For this the people were glad to give them six and eightpence a week.

Things went on like this until Arn, the old one, fell ill.

"One quarter of this moon belongs to me," said he, "and, if I die, I must have it to take to the grave with me."

When Arn died, the Mayor climbed up the tree
and snipped off one quarter of the moon with his
hedge shears. As Arn's property, this was put in the
coffin with him and buried.

The moon now gave a little less light, but still the nights were bright enough. Then, not long afterwards, Bor fell ill, and he too claimed a quarter of the moon as his share. So when Bor died, once more the Mayor climbed up the tree and cut off a second quarter of the moon with his hedge shears, and this was buried in Bor's coffin.

The light of the moon grew less; and it grew still less when Cass died, and the third quarter was cut off and placed in his coffin. Finally, when Deol died and took his quarter with

him, there was no moon at all. The old state of darkness began again, and the people of Exe, if they went out at night without their lanterns, bumped their heads together.

But in the land below the earth, where dead men
go and where it is always dark, the four pieces of
the moon joined together. In the soft light, which

now shone all the time, the dead began to feel
restless. Astonished to find they could see again, they
climbed out of their graves and were merry.

They began to behave as before, dancing, singing and gathering in the taverns to drink and jest. As you can imagine, they drank too much, for they had long

been unaccustomed to wine and ale. Some started
to brawl and quarrel. They took up cudgels and
began to attack each other.

The noise from the underworld grew louder and
louder, and at last reached heaven. On hearing it,
Saint Peter, who guards the gate of heaven, thought
that a state of war must have broken out in the
lower world. He summoned the Blessed Ones, whose
duty it was to drive off the assaults of the Evil One.

But the Blessed Ones did not come, so Saint Peter in a rage mounted his horse and rode out through the gate of heaven. He charged down to the lower world and, in a voice of thunder, ordered the dead to behave themselves and return to their graves.

He saw that the moon was the cause of all the trouble,
so he slung it over his back, galloped off and hung it
up in heaven; there, to this very day, it shines as
brightly as ever.

Printed in Great Britain by Butler & Tanner Ltd., Frome and London